Other books about the Church Mice are:

The Church Mouse
The Church Cat Abroad
The Church Mice and the Moon
The Church Mice Spread Their Wings
The Church Mice Adrift
The Church Mice at Bay
The Church Mice at Christmas

Also by Graham Oakley

Magical Changes
Hetty and Harriet

THE CHURCH MICE IN ACTION

Graham Oakley

Atheneum   New York

The Church Mice in Action
Copyright © 1982 by Graham Oakley

Library of Congress Cataloging in Publication Data

Oakley, Graham.
The church mice in action.

Summary: The Church mice enter Samson in a cat show to
win money to fix the church roof, but in doing so, they
unknowingly put him in danger.
(1. Mice—Fiction) I. Title.
PZ7.01048Cfj   1983   (E)   82-11394
ISBN 0-689-30949-X

First American Edition 1983

Printed by New Interlitho, Milan

One day, quite late in the summer, the church mice and Sampson the church cat were taking it easy in the churchyard. They were in a really mellow mood. But then Humphrey, who was a bit of a pessimist, said through a mouthful of blackberry that late summer was almost early winter and as the vestry roof was as leaky as ever the near future looked pretty wet and shivery. Somehow the mood wasn't quite as mellow after that.

There were two other people in the churchyard. One was the parson and the other was his sister who was spending a couple of weeks with him.

The parson was telling his sister all about squinch arches and crockets and things and she was telling him all about her best friend's new hat when suddenly she saw Sampson.

NOTICES

ST JOHN'S
VESTRY ROOF
FUND

£10,000 TARGET

DEAR PARISHIONERS
ONLY
£9,987.3½p
TO GO!
JOLLY GOOD
SHOW, KEEP
UP THE GOOD
WORK!
Rev R. Simpkins
Rector of...

THANK
YOU

Sampson was dreaming about the lovely times he used to have before he took his vow never to catch mice when a strange noise woke him up. It sounded something like, "Whoooose a booooooooooooooooooootiful puddy tat den. Come to mummmmy." He opened his eyes and saw an awesome sight.

"Roderick dear, he simply must come and stay at the vicarage," the parson's sister said to the parson. And without more ado she bore Sampson off.

Next morning Arthur and Humphrey went across to the vicarage just to make sure that Sampson was all right

and they were pleased to find that he was being looked after very, very well indeed.

After that they went back to the churchyard
and joined the other mice who were breakfasting
on something lovely that had been thrown over
the wall during the night. Arthur was on his
third chip when his eye fell on the ad. The idea
it gave him was so brilliant that he had to
swallow two more chips very quickly to calm his
nerves. Then he informed Humphrey that the
vestry roof problem was solved once and for all.

WORTLETHORPE CLARION

CAT LOVERS!
ENTER YOUR CAT IN THE
WORTLETHORPE LADIES' INSTITUTE
CAT SHOW
Big prizes to be won for the
PRETTIEST CAT; CLEVEREST CAT;
BEST GROOMED CAT; CAT WITH THE
LONGEST TAIL; CAT WITH BEST
BIGGEST EYES; CAT WITH BEST TRICKS
OWERS; CAT WITH BEST TRICKS
HALL at 10ᵃᵐ 10 SEPT 1982

Humphrey only really liked ideas he'd thought of himself so he looked
very doubtful and said that Sampson couldn't win anything except
booby prizes. Arthur said that that was true as far as
Handsomeness and Cleverness and Trick-performingness and
Well-bredness were concerned but after what they had
seen at the vicarage he thought Sampson would knock
spots off all comers in the Well-groomed department.
Humphrey just grunted but he agreed to write
the letter to the parson's sister explaining
the plan because only he knew the correct
way of addressing important people.

CAT LOVERS!
ENTER YOUR CAT IN THE
BARTLETHORPE LADIES IN...
CAT SHOW
prizes to be won
FINEST CAT: CL
GROOMED

the Vestri
St John's Church
Wartletnorpe
8th Sept Annie Domino 1962

Deer Miss, MADAM, Mrs or Ms
We Humbli beseech yu to BISToe
Your Esteeemed Atenshun
on the INKlosed advertisMUNT
Wee think that now yu
have refurbished BUN-UP
BAB BUB
PROBBERLEY win the "BEST GROOMED CAT"
prize in the CAT SHOW. The
ENORMOUS amount of prize
muni cud then BEE spent on mending
the VESTRI RUUF witch now LEEKS off
the obseqious HEDS of Your OBEDIENT
and RESPEKFULL SERVUNTS
Humprey & Arthur

SAMWm
CUTHBRT
Tom CREY
Minnie
HARRI
Archibald
Jane
Hannibal
Pea?c?

Parson's sister

The parson's sister was a bit put out at being written to by a pack of mice but the
parson made her see reason. He said that if he relied on the charity of his
fellow men the vestry roof wouldn't be mended until the middle of the twenty-
third century, so why not give the mice a chance?

So Sampson was entered for the Best Groomed Cat prize, and on the day of the cat show the mice were there to see him arrive. They hadn't intended to come because of the number of cats present but Humphrey worked out a plan to make certain that Sampson won and they had to be there to carry it out. Arthur had objected to the plan, using words like "un-sporting" and "downright un-British", and Humphrey had stood up for his plan, saying things about "mealy-mouthed hypocrites" and "nambypamby do-gooders". Humphrey had won the day.

The mayor opened the cat show with a little speech. He began by saying that since the time of Dick Whittington mayors and cats had gone together like fish and chips and the only reason why he didn't have a cat himself was because his wife was frightened of getting cat fleas in her fur coats. He ended by patting the first contestant on the head. Or rather he would have done if the mice hadn't put their plan into operation.

The plan was very simple, though it called for the most steely-nerved of the mice to carry it out.

And the plan's success depended on Sampson doing absolutely nothing. He did it perfectly.

So the judge had no choice but to award Sampson first prize. The mayor presented the prizes and he had intended to make another speech but he didn't because the only words that came into his head were things like "devilish fiends", "furies from Hell" and "ravaging beasts" and he didn't really think that would make him very popular with cat-loving voters.

After his success Sampson was entered in other cat shows and, with the aid of the mice, his prizes soon amounted to ten pounds, a year's supply of cat litter and three dozen boxes of flea powder. Humphrey claimed all the credit. "Chaps like me and Attila the Hun," he said, "just stick our hands in the World's Pocket and take what we want." Arthur said he supposed you *could* describe swindling fairly honest folk like that. All the other mice just called him a ninny so he didn't say any more. Next morning there was an article about Sampson in the paper. The mice read it with great interest . . .

. . . and so did some other people.

Later that day Sampson managed to give the parson's sister the slip. The first thing he did after escaping was to get rid of his horrible bow.

He was so absorbed in doing this that he didn't notice the danger until it was too late.

Next day a ransom note arrived at the vicarage. The parson's sister, upset as she was, was glad to see the kidnappers had done it correctly, just like on TV.

We HAVE the cat. Put ALL his Stupendous Winnings! in a Pork bAg and leave in THE under the NEW statue at 10 A.M. tomorrow or YOU will NEVER C him AGAIN GOOD

It will BEANO telling the POLICE because WE R 2 smart 2 B caught Must rush NOW 2 catch THE post CeRely

One of his whiskers TO prove THAT we HAVE him

YOURS CuRly Dumble CHARley Numbskill 2 PLANK street Wortlethorpe

They did exactly what the note demanded except that they couldn't find a sack big enough to hold all the cat litter. They did manage to get in all the flea powder though. They were sad about the ten pound note but, as they said, Sampson's life was worth that. While they were getting the wheelbarrow Arthur and Humphrey strolled by, and being nosey they just had to have a peep in the sack

And before they knew where they were they'd been delivered with the ransom. They just managed to jump out of the sack before the kidnappers arrived. The first thing they noticed when they were safe on the ground were some funny Sampson-type noises which they tracked down while the kidnappers were deciding who should open the sack.

Some things the kidnappers weren't very good at, but doing up straps wasn't one of them.

The mice were still struggling with it when the kidnappers at last got themselves sorted out and made their getaway. The two men were very angry. They knew Sampson had won thousands because they read it in the papers and they weren't going to let him go for a measly ten pounds and some second-hand flea powder.

The mice didn't know exactly what was going on but they did know that their ten pound prize shouldn't be in someone else's pocket.

So they removed it. Then Humphrey popped up aloft to see where they were going. But before he had time to find his bearings he lost his footing.

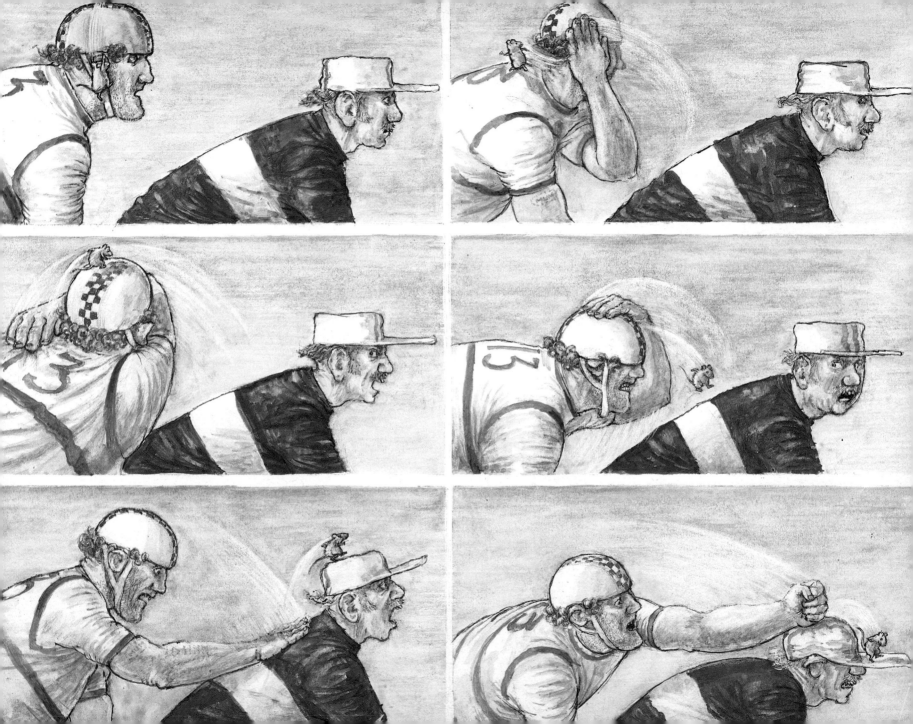

Everybody was still for a while, wondering which bit of himself was broken. The ten pound note was the first to move, followed closely by Arthur and Humphrey.

The ten pound note had the advantage in the race. The mice and men were pretty evenly matched.

What the kidnappers gained by length of leg the mice made up for by shortness of leg.

Humphrey gasped peevishly that it was disgusting what humans would go through just to get their

hands on mere money. Arthur, wet, puffed, pricked, and stung, just sniffed as sarcastically as shortage of breath would allow.

Then, just when everybody thought the money was within their grasp, their hopes went up in smoke.

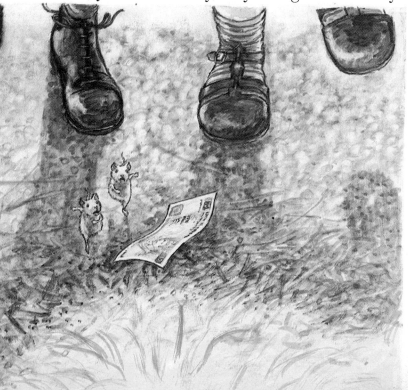

For a few moments everyone's feelings got the better of them.

After that the mice set off home. They would have forgotten all about Sampson if they hadn't come upon the kidnappers again and stopped to listen to them out of curiosity. Most of the noises the men were making weren't exactly words but what words they did say were about all the nasty things they were going to do to Sampson, whom they blamed for all their troubles. At that the mice quickened their pace because they knew that if Sampson was to get much older they must reach him first.

They did get to Sampson first, but the plastic string around the box was too tough for their teeth. They just had time to gnaw holes for his legs in the bottom of the box before the kidnappers arrived.

When the kidnappers saw that the box containing Sampson had vanished they did three things. Firstly, they remembered all the swear words they'd ever known. Secondly, they started to search for the box . . .

. . . and thirdly, they set an unofficial world tandem speed record over twenty-three miles.

Getting home could have been a problem, but luck was with them. Soon Sampson was unpacked and they were bowling along in comfort. Humphrey said, though not in so many words, that now they had taught the kidnappers that crime didn't pay they could get back to rigging the cat shows and make themselves a fortune. But Arthur and Sampson gave him a look that would have made even a hero's knees knock.

So there were no more cat shows. A few days later the parson's sister went home and soon after that the last whiffs of Magnolia Blossom faded out of Sampson's fur and the mice stopped holding their noses when they came near him. The vestry roof leaked more than ever but the verger kept the stove going day and night to make up for it. And with bits of the parish magazine stuffed in the cracks around the windows and a few hassocks along the bottom of the doors to keep out the draughts, the mice could doze cosily around the stove on winter evenings while Humphrey told them for the hundredth time about how he had outwitted the kidnappers.